The Boy Who Cried Wolf

with
The Goose That Laid the Golden Eggs

Illustrated by Val Biro

D1479942

Award Publications Limited

There was once a boy who had a flock of sheep. All day long he watched over them, but nothing ever happened.

The villagers told
the boy to shout for help
if he saw a wolf. But he never
saw one. He was very bored.

One day the boy had an idea.

"Wolf! Wolf!"
he cried.
The men from the
village ran up the hill to
chase the wolf away.

But the men saw no wolf. So they went back to the village.

"We must have scared it away," said one man.

The boy laughed. He thought he was very clever to trick the men.

The next day the boy played the same trick. "Wolf! Wolf!" he shouted at the top of his voice.

Once again, the villagers ran to help. They yelled and waved sticks and swords.

Once again, the men did not see a wolf. But they did see the little boy laughing at them.

"You will cry wolf once too often," warned the eldest man. But the boy just laughed.

After a while the boy became
tired of his trick. For a time
things were quiet in the village.

Then one day a real wolf did
appear. It was very hungry.
It snapped its teeth at the boy.

The boy ran to the village as fast as he could. "Wolf! Wolf!" he cried. "Wolf! Wolf!"

But the villagers ignored him.
They thought he was playing a
trick on them again.

The wolf ate up all the sheep. The boy learned a lesson that day. He never told a lie again.

The Goose That Laid the Golden Eggs

An old man and an old woman lived in an old house. They were very poor. They had nothing but a white goose.

One day the goose laid an egg. It had never laid an egg before. The egg was made of gold!

"It is solid gold!" cried the old man. "We will be the richest people in the village!"

They danced and cheered.

The next day the goose laid another golden egg. But the old man and the old woman became greedy.

"It will take a long time to become rich if we get only one egg a day," said the old woman. "Let's cut open the goose and have all the golden eggs at once!"

So they did just that. But they found that the goose was not filled with golden eggs at all.

The old man and the old woman had been too greedy. Now they had no more golden eggs and no goose.